OCT 16

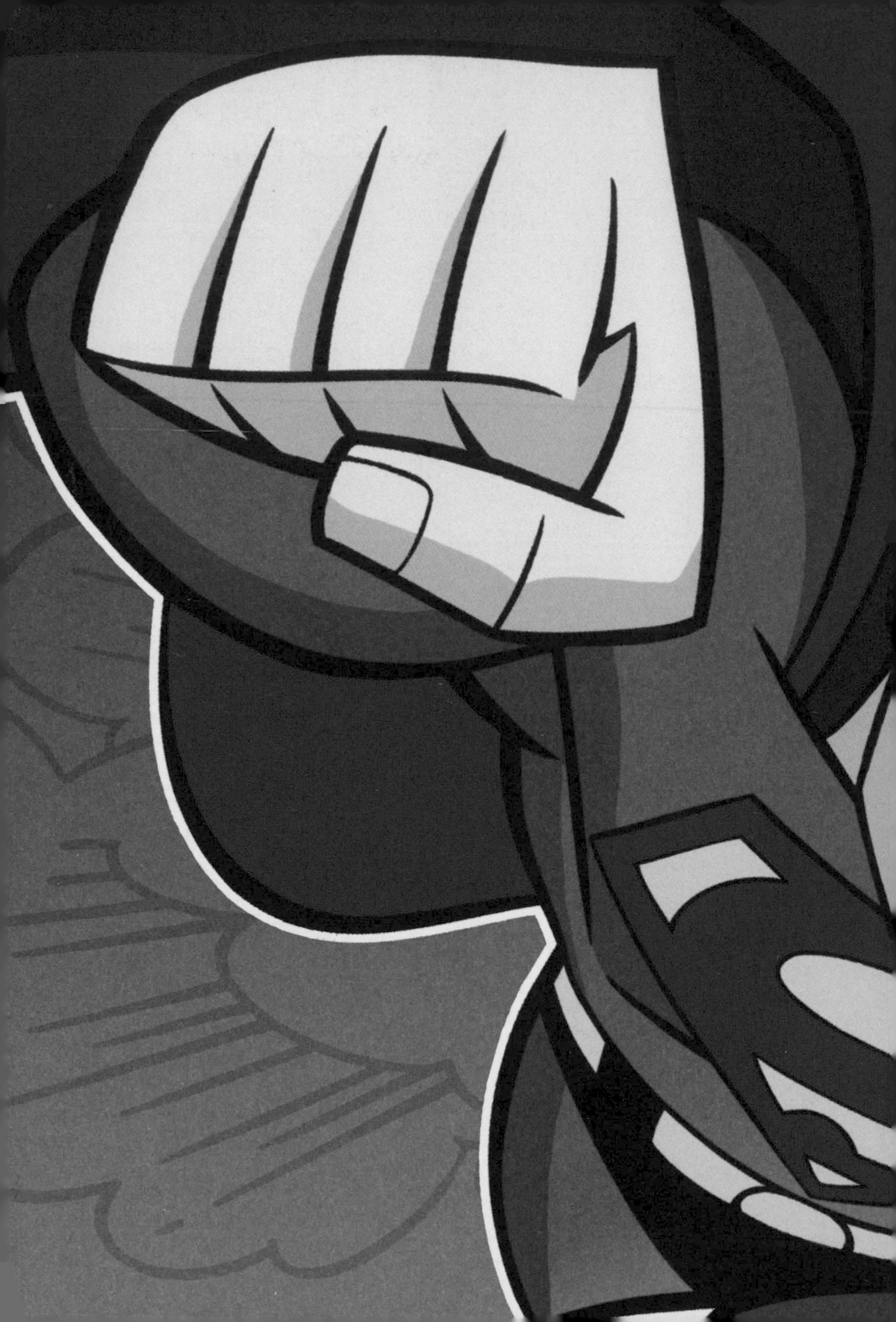

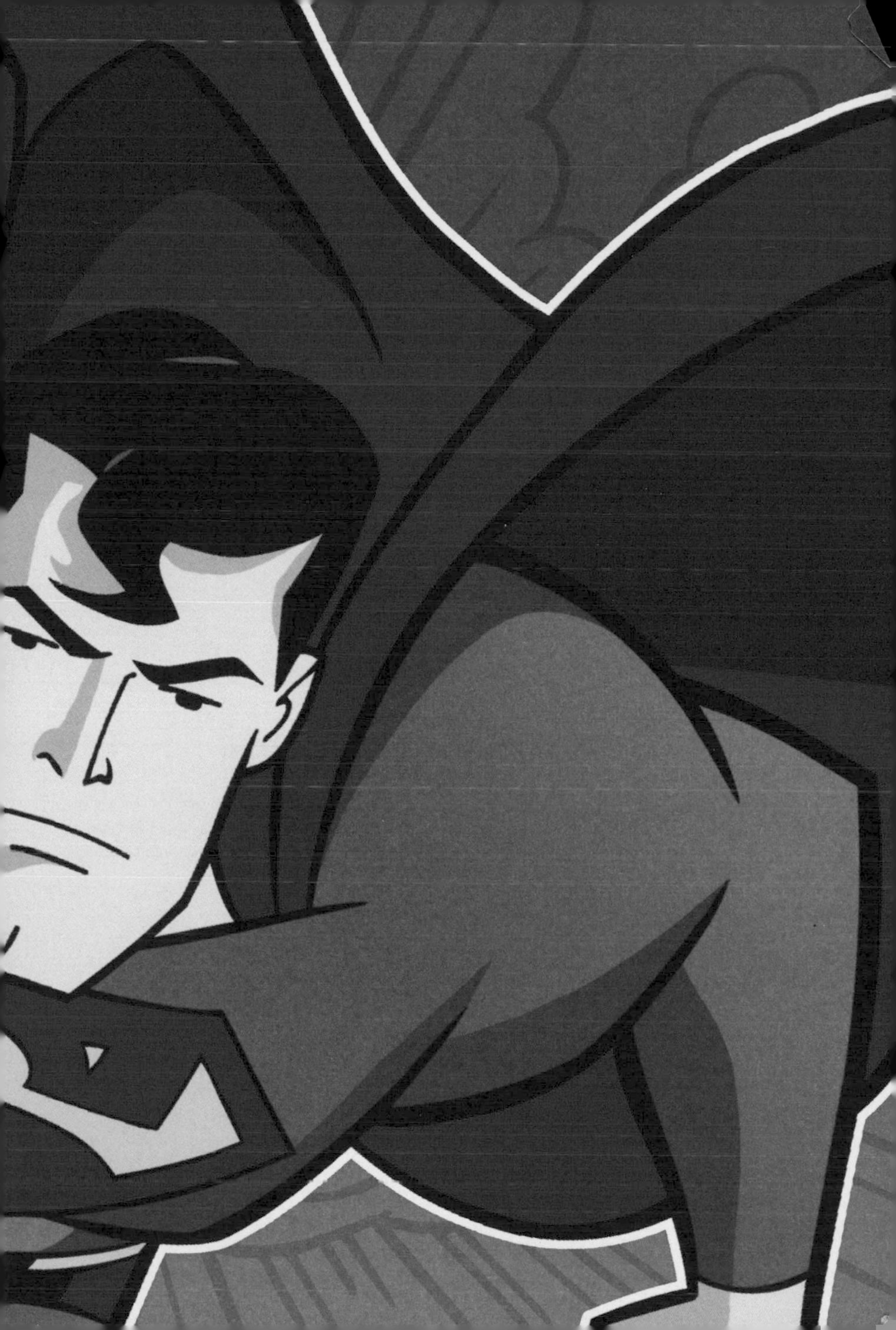

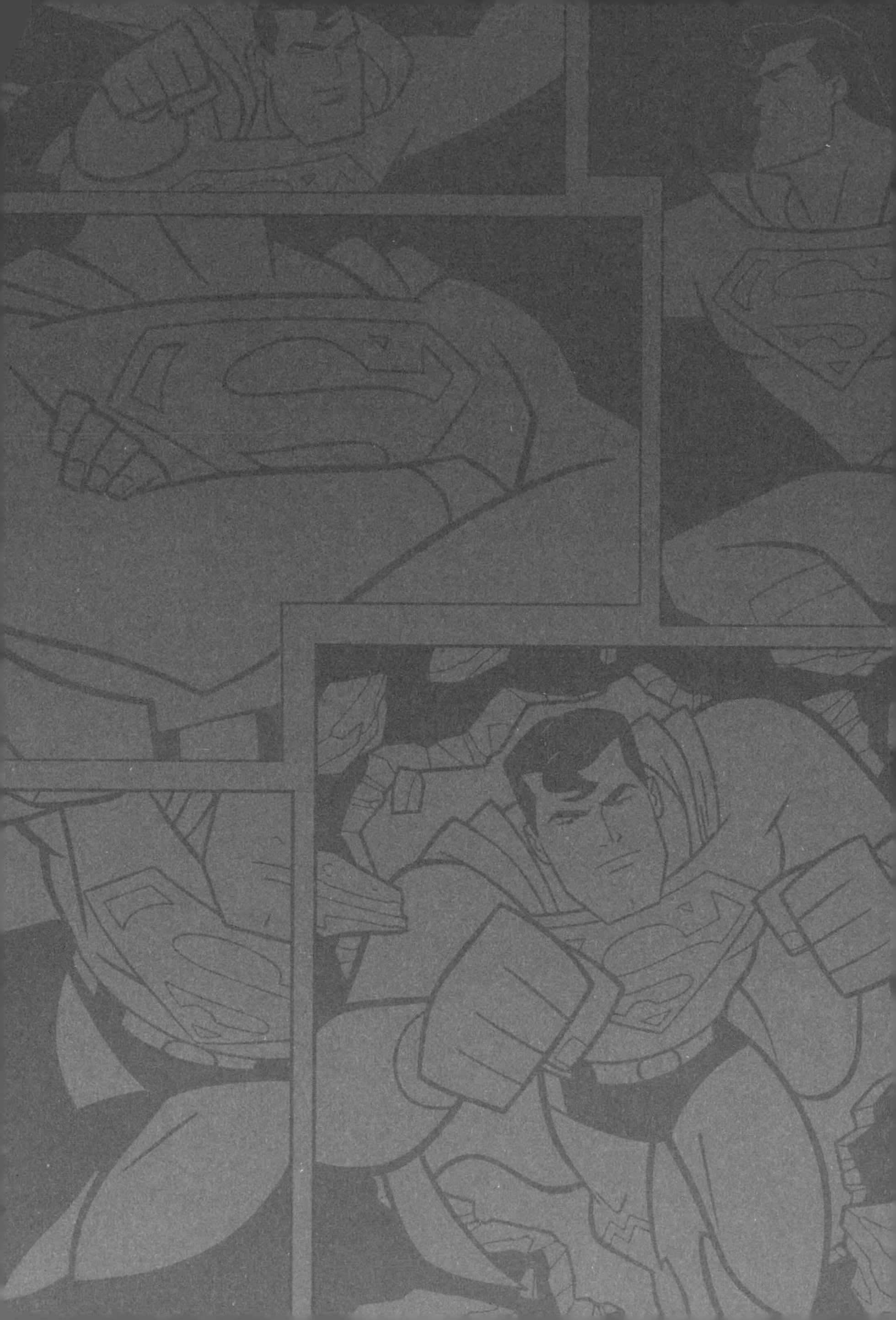

DC COMICS™
SUPER HEROES

SUPERMAN™

THE SHADOW MASTERS

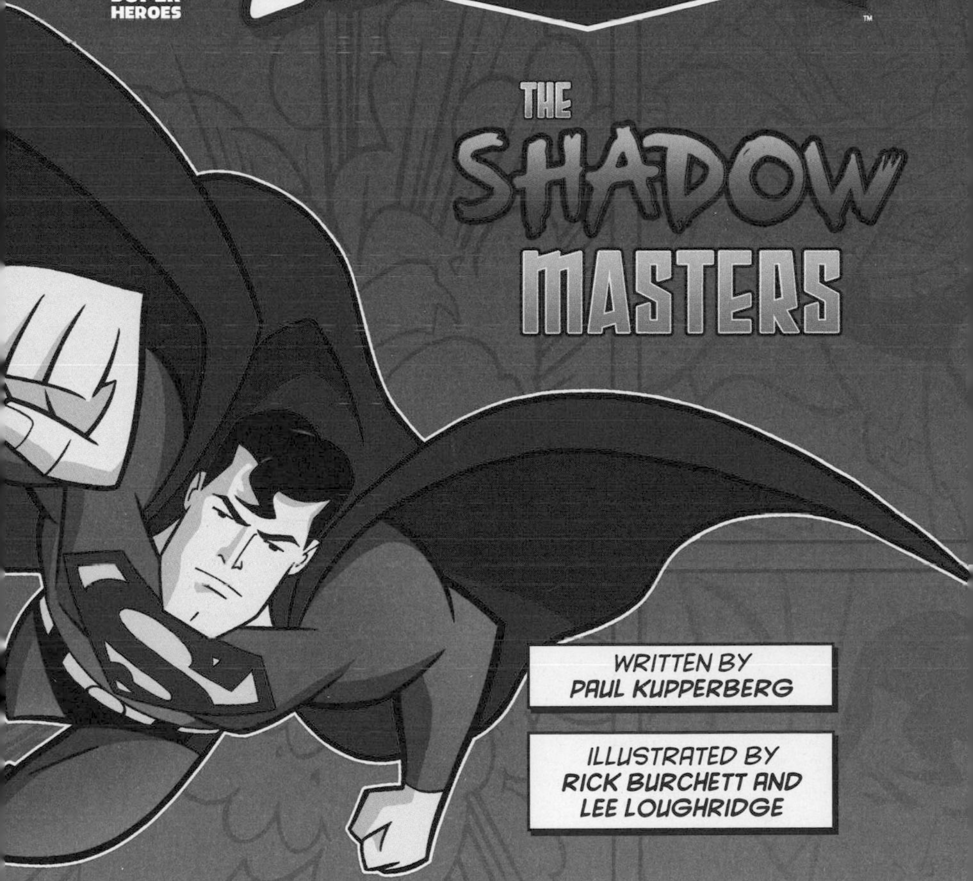

WRITTEN BY
PAUL KUPPERBERG

ILLUSTRATED BY
RICK BURCHETT AND
LEE LOUGHRIDGE

SUPERMAN CREATED BY
JERRY SIEGEL AND
JOE SHUSTER
BY SPECIAL ARRANGEMENT WITH
THE JERRY SIEGEL FAMILY

STONE ARCH BOOKS
a capstone imprint

Published by Stone Arch Books
A Capstone Imprint
1710 Roe Crest Drive
North Mankato, Minnesota 56003
www.capstonepub.com

STAR13260

Cataloging-in-Publication Data is available on the Library of Congress
website.

ISBN: 978-1-4342-2079-0 (library binding)
ISBN: 978-1-4342-2768-3 (paperback)

Summary: When the electricity in Metropolis suddenly goes out, Superman
quickly locates the problem. It's Acrata, a super heroine who can teleport
through shadows. She insists that the power must be shut down, or the
planet will be doomed. Superman isn't convinced. He stops Acrata, but
soon a new problem arrives. The evil Eclipso appears, threatening to take
over the world! Superman and Acrata must stop him from casting an evil
shadow over Earth.

Art Director: Bob Lentz
Designer: Hilary Wacholz
Production Specialist: Michelle Biedscheid

Printed in the United States of America in Stevens Point, Wisconsin.
112013
007879R

TABLE OF CONTENTS

CHAPTER 1

THE MISSING ROCKS 4

CHAPTER 2

SHORT-CIRCUIT. 13

CHAPTER 3

INSIDE THE SHADOWS 21

CHAPTER 4

INTO THE LIGHT. 29

CHAPTER 5

POWER SURGE. 38

THE MISSING ROCKS

"It doesn't make sense," said Detective Bill Henderson of the Metropolis Police Department. "Why would someone break into a museum filled with priceless artifacts and only steal a few small diamonds?"

"I was just about to ask you the same question," replied newspaper reporter Clark Kent. "Are you sure that's all they took?"

The detective nodded. "And we still can't figure out how the robber got in here," he said. "The theft wasn't discovered until the museum opened this morning."

The geology exhibit was on the top floor of the Metropolis Museum of Natural History. A glass display case held samples of common rocks, minerals, and jewels. Small labels identified each sample as granite, iron, lead, or nickel. There was a blank space beside the label for black diamonds. Those samples were gone!

As a reporter for the *Daily Planet*, Clark had covered many robberies. He had seen jewelry stores where millions of dollars in gold had been taken. He had also written stories about stickups in grocery markets where robbers had gotten away with less than one hundred dollars. No matter what was taken, something of value had always been stolen. But compared to other items in the museum, the black diamonds weren't very valuable.

"What do you know about similar thefts of black diamonds from other Metropolis museums?" asked Clark.

Detective Henderson scowled. He shoved his hands into the pockets of his trench coat. "Why would someone go through so much trouble to steal a few rocks?" he said. "Those things must have some sort of special value."

"I think you're right," said Clark. "I think these black diamonds must be very valuable . . . to somebody."

"If you find out who," the detective replied, "let me know."

A short time later, Clark exited the museum. He tucked his notepad into his pocket and then checked his watch. The robbery wasn't his only assignment today.

Clark also had to report on a rare solar eclipse. He was scheduled to be at the Weisinger Observatory at Metropolis State University. The sky would begin darkening in less than half an hour.

The mystery of the black diamonds troubled the reporter as he walked away from the museum. The rocks had to be important to someone . . . but who?

RUMMMMMMMMMBLE! Clark was only slightly aware of a distant tremor. He was lost in thoughts of mysterious jewels and unknown crooks. At first he thought the noise was from an approaching storm. But he quickly realized that the rumbling was not coming from the sky. It was coming from beneath his feet!

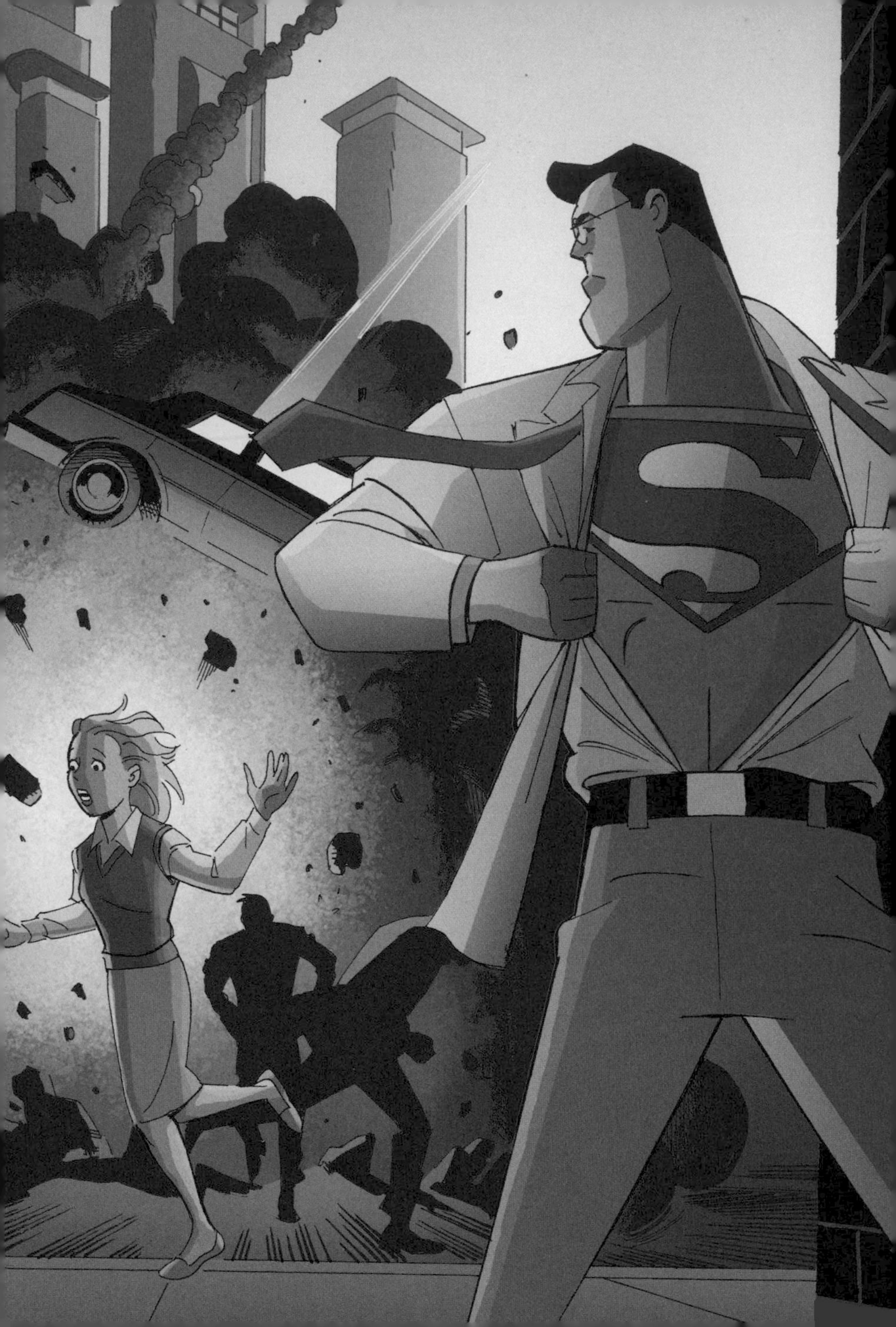

With an ear-splitting roar, a series of underground explosions rocked the streets. One. Two. Three. Four. Five. The explosions were coming closer and closer. Electrical sparks and flames erupted from below. Manhole covers burst into the air.

What's happening? wondered Clark. He took off his glasses. In a moment, the reporter was gone. He had changed into Superman, the mighty Man of Steel.

WHOOOOSH!

Superman flew skyward. A blue and red streak zigzagged through the air. The figure snatched the manhole covers in flight. Electrical sparks flared for a moment from the manholes. The air smelled of burned plastic and rubber. Traffic lights began to flicker. Then suddenly, they went out. Stores and buildings went dark.

Superman landed and safely stacked the manhole covers on the street. He narrowed his eyes. Using his X-ray vision, he looked through the pavement to the tunnels below. Peering through telephone wires, power lines, and sewer pipes, he saw that several electrical transformers had exploded. These devices changed high-voltage electricity into a lower-voltage electricity. Without them, homes and businesses would be blacked out.

"What could have caused those explosions?" Superman said to himself.

Just then, from out of the inky shadows of a nearby alley, a figure dressed in a hooded black and green jumpsuit appeared. She seemed to slither out of the shadows themselves, as if she was part of the dark.

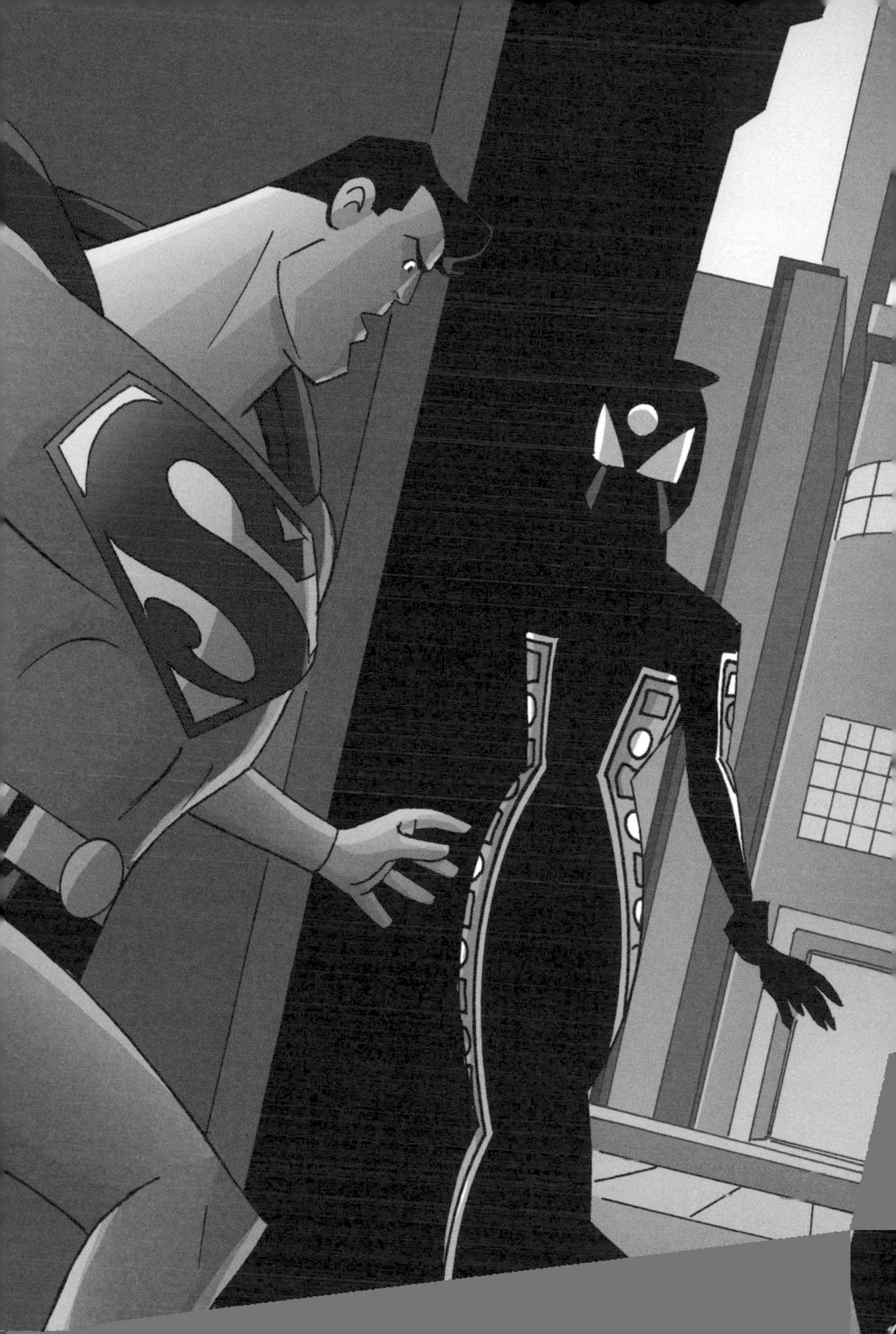

"Acrata!" Superman exclaimed. "I'm glad you're here. I could use some help finding out who caused these explosions."

"I can help you with that question," said Acrata, the mysterious super hero from Mexico. "*I* did it!"

CHAPTER 2

SHORT-CIRCUIT

"You?" asked Superman. "But why?"

Just then, a policewoman came running toward him. She held a radio in her hand.

"Superman!" the officer shouted. "The whole west side of the city has gone dark. The power company says the blackout started nearby."

"You'd better have a good explanation for this, Acrata," Superman said.

Acrata nodded. She took a step back toward the shadow of the alley.

"Beware of the Man in the Shadows," Acrata warned. "When the sun is eclipsed, he will destroy the Heart of Darkness. Then he will make Earth his own!" With that, the hero disappeared back into the alley.

What did she mean? Superman wondered. *Why does Acrata want to darken the streets of Metropolis? She's known to be good, not evil.*

Acrata was Andrea Rojas, a professor of ancient South and Central American cultures at a university in Mexico. As a child, she had gained the power to teleport in and out of the shadows. Acrata used that power to fight crime. She helped protect Mexico, as well as the United States.

After Acrata had disappeared, Superman walked toward the front of the museum. "Who is the 'Man in the Shadows?'" he asked himself.

Inspector Henderson emerged from the blacked-out museum. He was closing his cell phone and looked worried.

"Superman!" he shouted. "A call just came in from the north side power station. A woman wearing black is trying to destroy their main generator!"

"I'm on my way, Inspector," Superman said. "But first, I need to warn the other power stations in town that they could be in danger."

WHOOOOSH! With a single leap, the Man of Steel took to the sky and was gone.

*   *   *

On the north end of Metropolis stood the Power and Light Substation. The building housed giant turbines that provided electricity for most of the city.

On a normal day, all that could be heard outside the power plant's concrete walls was the steady hum of electricity. Today, the gentle whir of the power lines was a high-pitched whine. As Superman flew closer to the building, it sounded as though the power plant was crying out in pain. Then from within, he heard the sound of muffled explosions.

KA-BOOM! KA-BOOM!

In the blink of an eye, the Man of Steel flew through an open window. Thick smoke poured out. The lights flickered in the vast room that housed the giant electric turbines. The machines themselves spun madly out of control. **BZZT! BZZT!** They sparked and spit flames.

At the center of the destruction was Acrata, racing between the turbines.

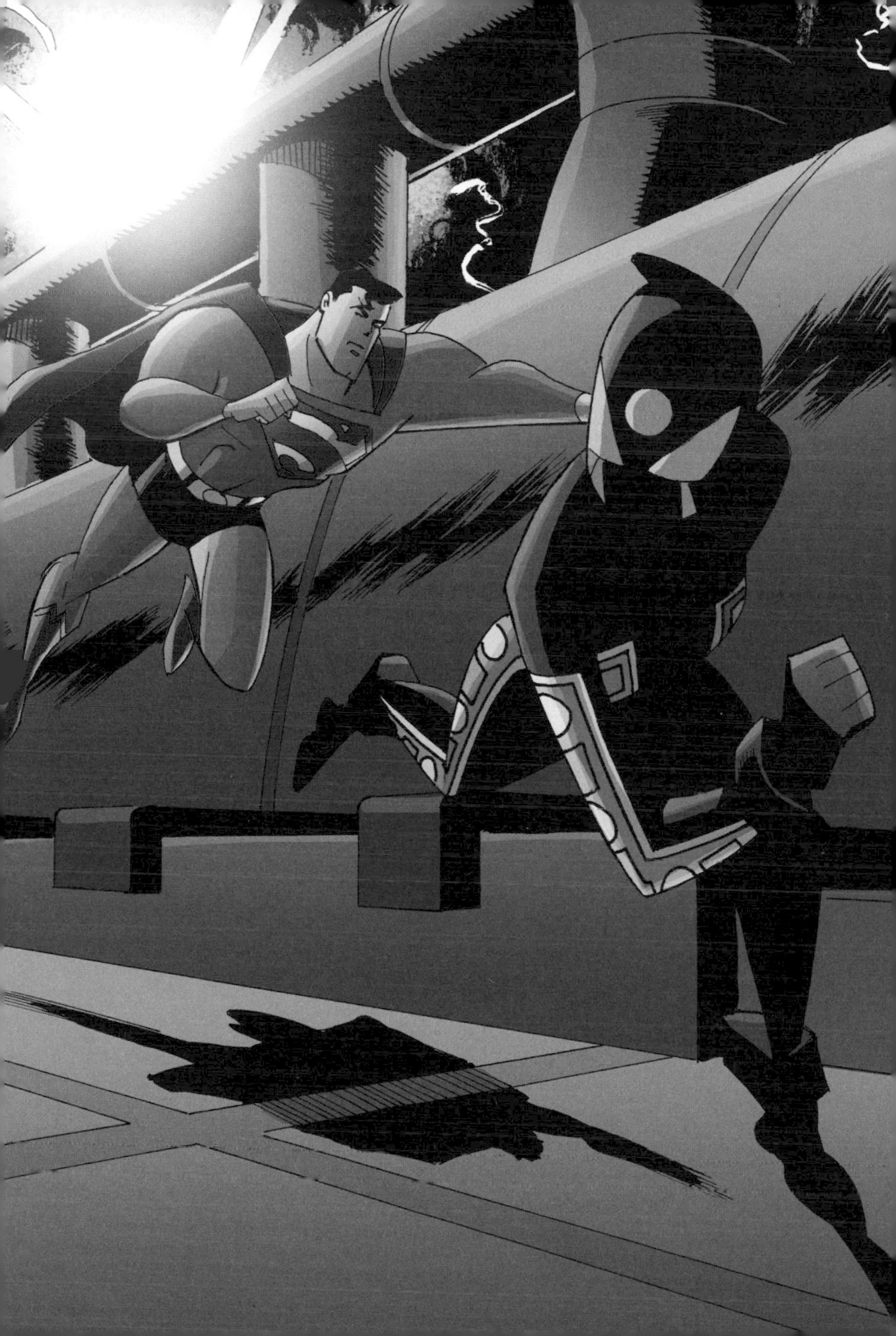

The Mexican super hero zigzagged through the high-voltage maze at lightning speed. Acrata ran toward a dark corner of the room. As soon as she entered the shadows, she could disappear and escape.

In a flash, Superman landed directly in front of her. **THUD!** He stood with his arms out, blocking her path.

"You must not stop me, Superman," she said. "The Man in the Shadows is hiding in the darkness! He's waiting to strike!"

"What shadow man?" asked Superman. "Slow down, Acrata. Can't we talk about the situation?"

"No!" Acrata cried. "The Man in the Shadows arrives soon! He will use this electricity to regain his evil superpowers. He will destroy Earth!"

Before Superman could ask what she meant, the damaged turbines finally shut down. The power station went black.

"So long, Superman," he heard Acrata say as she teleported away.

Several moments later, the emergency lights came on. The power company workers began to come out from hiding.

A man wearing a hard hat walked up to Superman. "Is it safe?" he asked.

"Yes, Acrata is gone," Superman answered. "Do you know how much damage was done?"

"A lot," said the man in the hard hat. "It's going to take several hours to get us up and running again."

"I'm sure you'll do your best," said the Man of Steel.

"Now please excuse me," the super hero added. "I have a job of my own to do!"

CHAPTER 3

INSIDE THE SHADOWS

THWOOOOMMM!! Superman flew from the power station. *In fact, I have two jobs to do!* he thought.

Clark Kent's interview with the scientists at the Weisinger Observatory about the solar eclipse would have to wait. He would cover that story later. Perry White, his editor at the *Daily Planet*, might be angry. But the story of Acrata's attack on the power stations would please him.

To write that story, Clark would need to find out *why* she was doing it!

Superman soared through the skies over Metropolis. As he flew, he scanned the streets below with his super-vision. Half of the city was blacked out. The police were in the streets, directing traffic on the roads. They made sure people were safe.

Acrata had started on the west side of Metropolis. Then she moved on to the north end. She seemed to be moving clockwise around the city. She was taking out one section of the electrical grid at a time.

"If I'm right," Superman said to himself, "she'll hit the east side power station next!"

As if in answer, a great cloud of black smoke erupted in the east. BOOM! Superman streaked toward the scene of the disaster. Then, in midair, the Man of Steel changed his course. He was now heading south.

*   *   *

Acrata moved from place to place through the shadows. It felt as though she was sliding through a warm fog. She could see where she had been, and where she was going. The rest of the shadow world that surrounded her was a dark haze.

Andrea Rojas had gained her amazing powers from an ancient stone symbol. It had been discovered by her father, a famous archaeologist. The symbol came from the Maya. They were a great civilization that had ruled parts of Central America for almost 3,000 years.

She had come to love the shadows, using them to escape any danger. She would enter a dark corner in her apartment in Mexico City. Seconds later, she could reappear in any shadow she wished.

Rojas decided to use this power to fight criminals and organized crime. She wanted to help people who could not help themselves. That is, until she learned that she was not alone in the shadows.

Acrata could not really see him, this Man in the Shadows. His black form blended perfectly into the darkness. It hid him from sight. But she could feel him out there . . . somewhere.

Acrata knew he had already visited Earth several times, but he only stayed for a few moments. The solar eclipse, however, would give the evildoer enough darkness to complete his ultimate task.

When the shadows fall, Acrata thought, *the super-villain will destroy the Heart of Darkness diamonds. Then he will regain his superpowers and blot out the sun forever!*

Time was growing short. Acrata didn't even have time to explain her actions to the Man of Steel. In minutes, it would be too late. Minutes were all she needed, however. When she stepped from the shadows, she would be inside the south side power station. Once she stopped those turbines, the city would be completely powerless. The Shadow Man would no longer have a source of energy strong enough to destroy the diamonds.

Acrata started to leave the darkness. She stepped onto the streets of Metropolis. Suddenly, a gloved hand reached from the haze, grabbing her arm.

"Pardon me," said a raspy voice. "Do you mind if I tag along?"

"Ah!" Acrata screamed in surprise. She tumbled from the darkness into the light.

* * *

Meanwhile, Superman flew toward southern Metropolis. At the same time, the Moon's shape began to overlap the edge of the sun. It would take about seven minutes for the shadow to cover the face of the sun completely. Then Metropolis would turn as dark as night. That would happen at exactly noon.

"I must stop her," Superman said to himself. "Otherwise, she will plunge the entire city into darkness!"

ZWWWOOOMMMM! Superman rocketed downward from the sky. He landed inside the gates of the south side power station. He raced through the doors. Using his super-vision, he looked for a sign of Acrata.

"Ah!" came a scream from behind him.

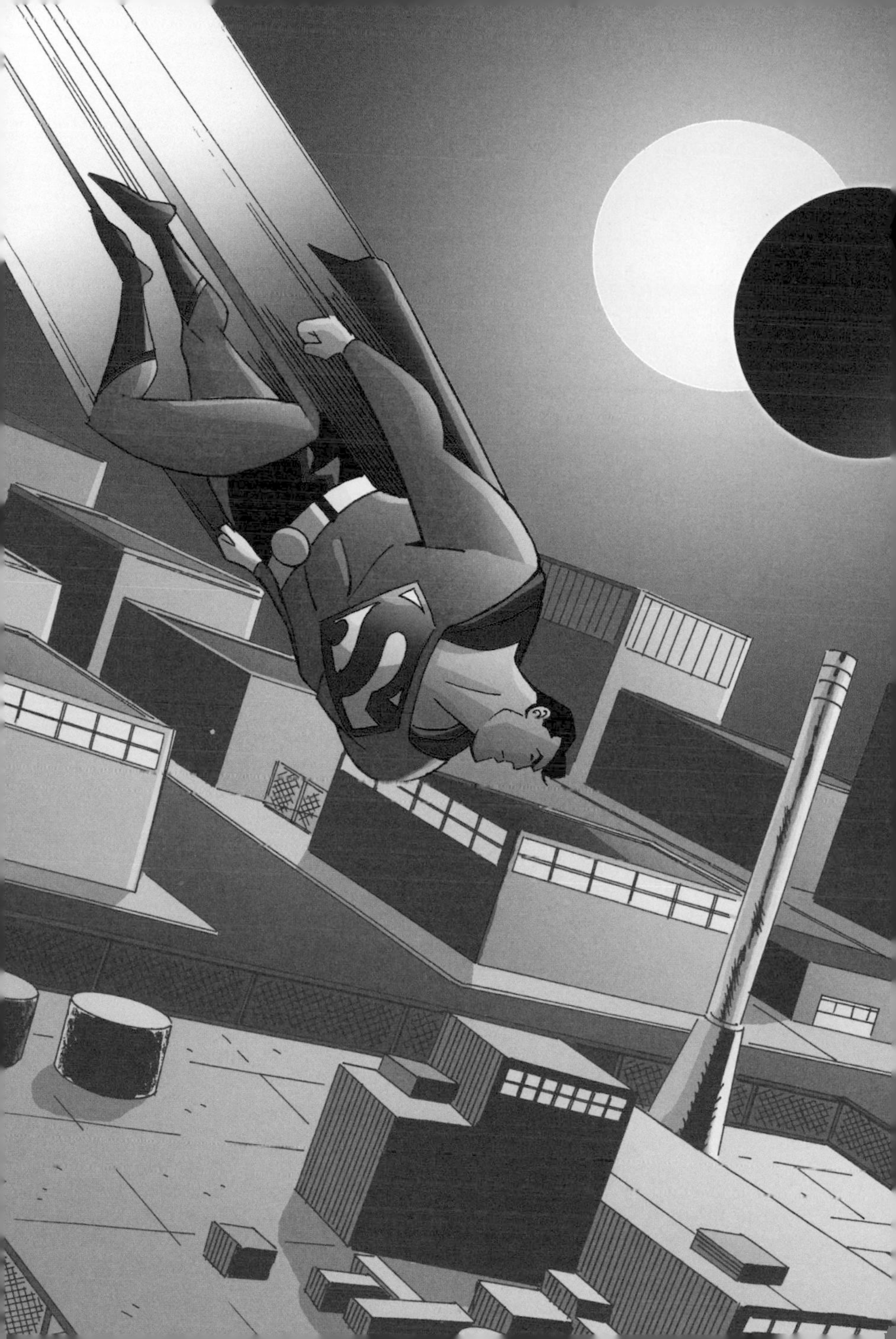

Superman whirled to face a pool of shadows under one of the turbines. The scream was coming from the darkness!

CHAPTER 4

INTO THE LIGHT

Before the Man of Steel could react, Acrata spilled from the shadows. She was kicking her legs as she dragged herself along the floor. It was like she was trying to break free from a trap. In an instant, Superman saw why. A hand in a dark purple glove had hold of one of her ankles!

"Superman!" Acrata cried when she saw the Man of Steel. "Help me!"

"Acrata, hold still!" the Man of Steel said. "He's using you to pull himself free of the shadows!"

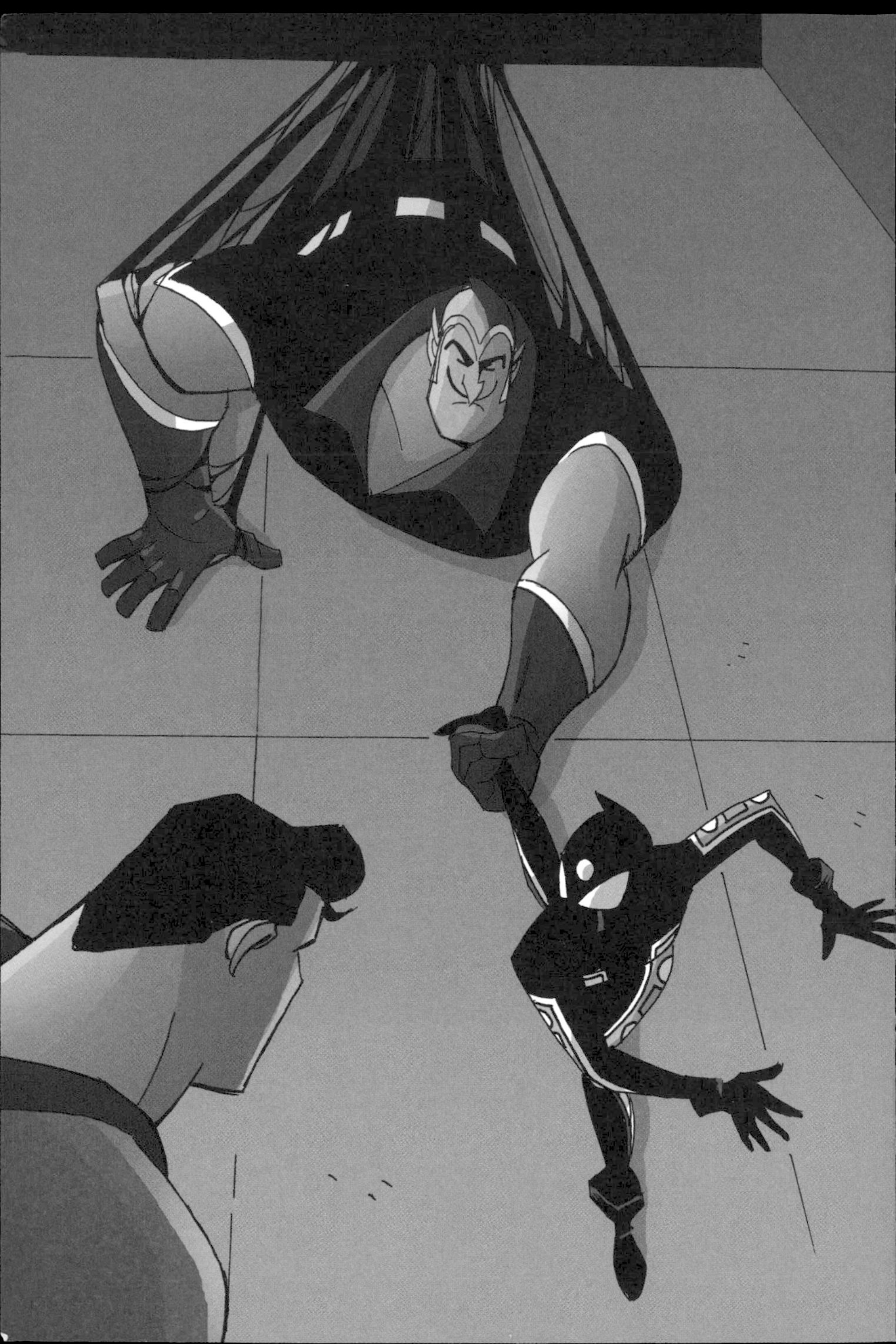

A second hand, in an identical glove, popped from the blackness. It grabbed one of the nearby rails of the metal safety fence around the turbine.

"Yesss!" said the voice.

He let go of Acrata's ankle. She then scrambled away, as if shot from a cannon.

The two hands grasped the fence. The villain let out a roar that sounded like an angry lion. ROOAAARRR!!

The man pulled himself out from the darkness. "Eclipso!" Superman gasped. The hulking figure in black and purple rose to his feet.

"You know this monster, Superman?" Acrata asked.

"We've met many times," said Eclipso.

"I've tried to spread my darkness across this little world before," said the villain. "Superman has always interfered."

"He's called Eclipso," said Superman. "His real name is Dr. Bruce Gordon, a scientist. He was observing a solar eclipse in the jungles of Central America when he was attacked by the sorcerer of a local tribe."

"Yes, yes," Eclipso interrupted. "The sorcerer scratched Gordon with his magical black diamond. Whenever there is an eclipse, I become Eclipso. When there is not an eclipse, I turn back into that goody-goody fool while Eclipso remains trapped in the shadows!"

"And you're going right back there," Superman said. "I see you don't have the black diamonds that hold your power."

"Oh, but I do, Superman," Eclipso said with a laugh.

The super-villain opened his fist. He showed the super heroes the dozens of small pieces of black diamonds he held.

"I had just enough power left to reach into this world," Eclipso said. "I was able to gather the scattered pieces of my shattered black jewels!"

"So you're the museum thief," Superman said.

"Guilty as charged," Eclipso admitted. "These black diamonds contain all of my superpowers. If the diamonds are destroyed, the powers will be set free. The world will be permanently covered in darkness. I will rule it all!"

"What have I done?" Acrata cried.

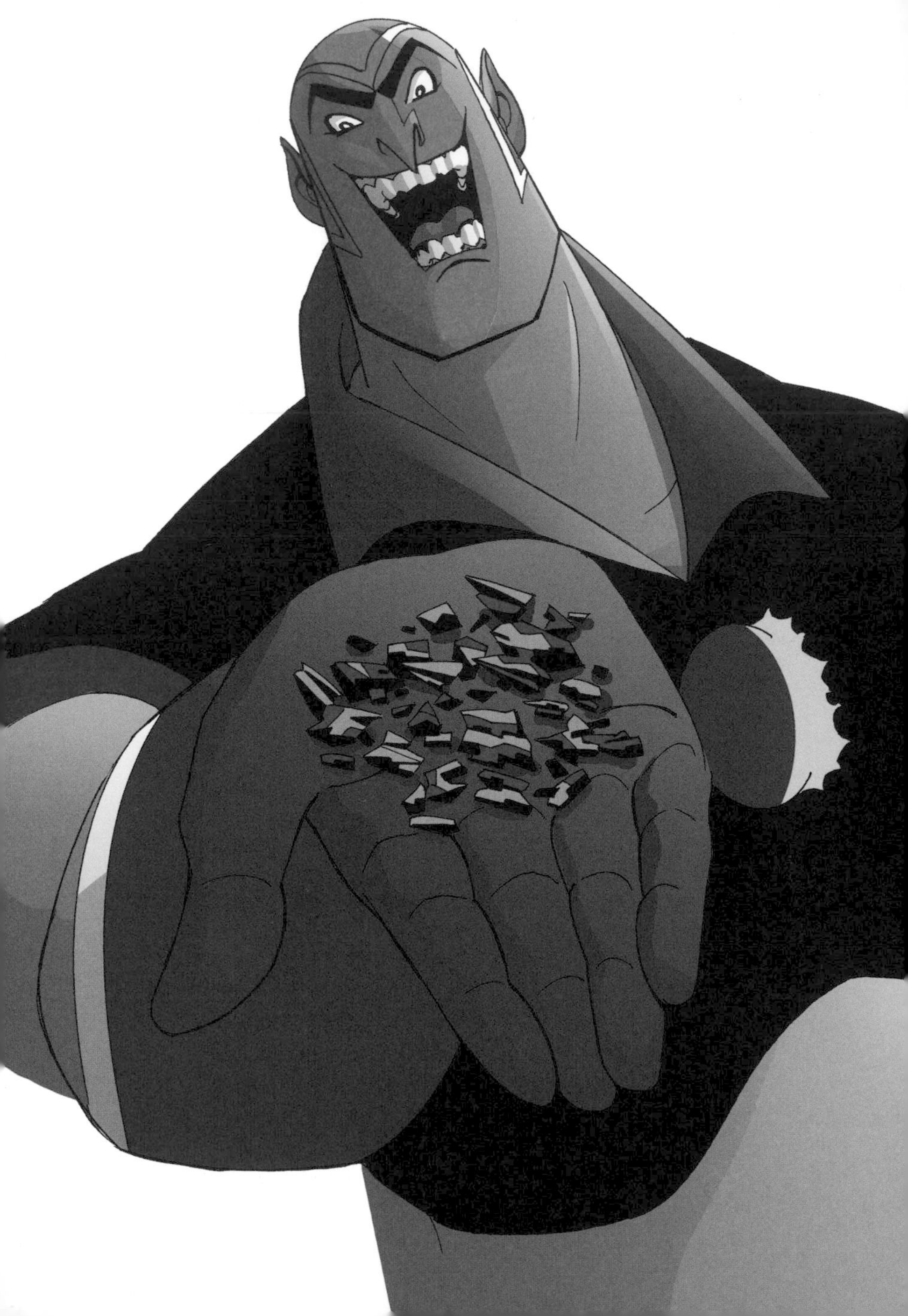

"I brought him to the real world from the shadows," continued Acrata. "I shut down all the electric plants. I thought that Eclipso wouldn't have enough energy to destroy the diamonds that way!"

"Never fear, Acrata," Superman said. "He's going right back into the darkness where he belongs!"

Eclipso's laugh echoed through the large space. "That's what you think, Man of Steel!" said the super-villain. "As we speak, the solar eclipse has reached totality. That is the moment when the face of the sun is totally covered by the shadow of the Moon. And it's the moment I have been waiting for!"

Eclipso closed his fingers around the pile of diamonds. He smashed his fist into the side of the spinning turbine. **CRASH!!**

BZZZT! The electrical power traveled up his arm and surged into Eclipso. His whole body sizzled and glowed with blue light.

Enough electricity to kill a thousand men coursed through his body. The villain threw back his head and laughed.

HAHAHAHA!

"Stand back!" the Man of Steel said. "This is a job for Superman!"

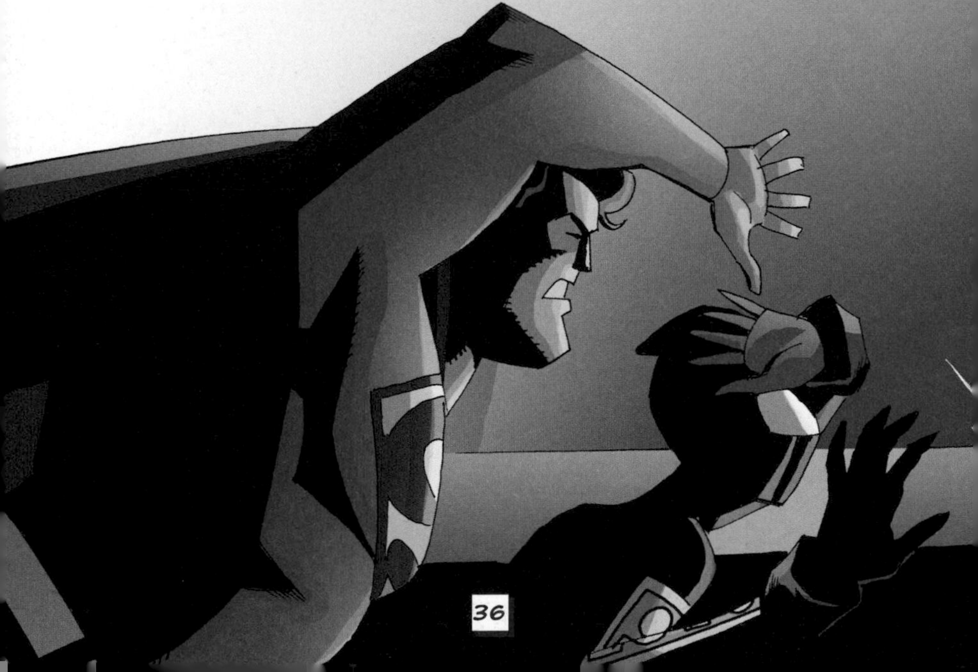

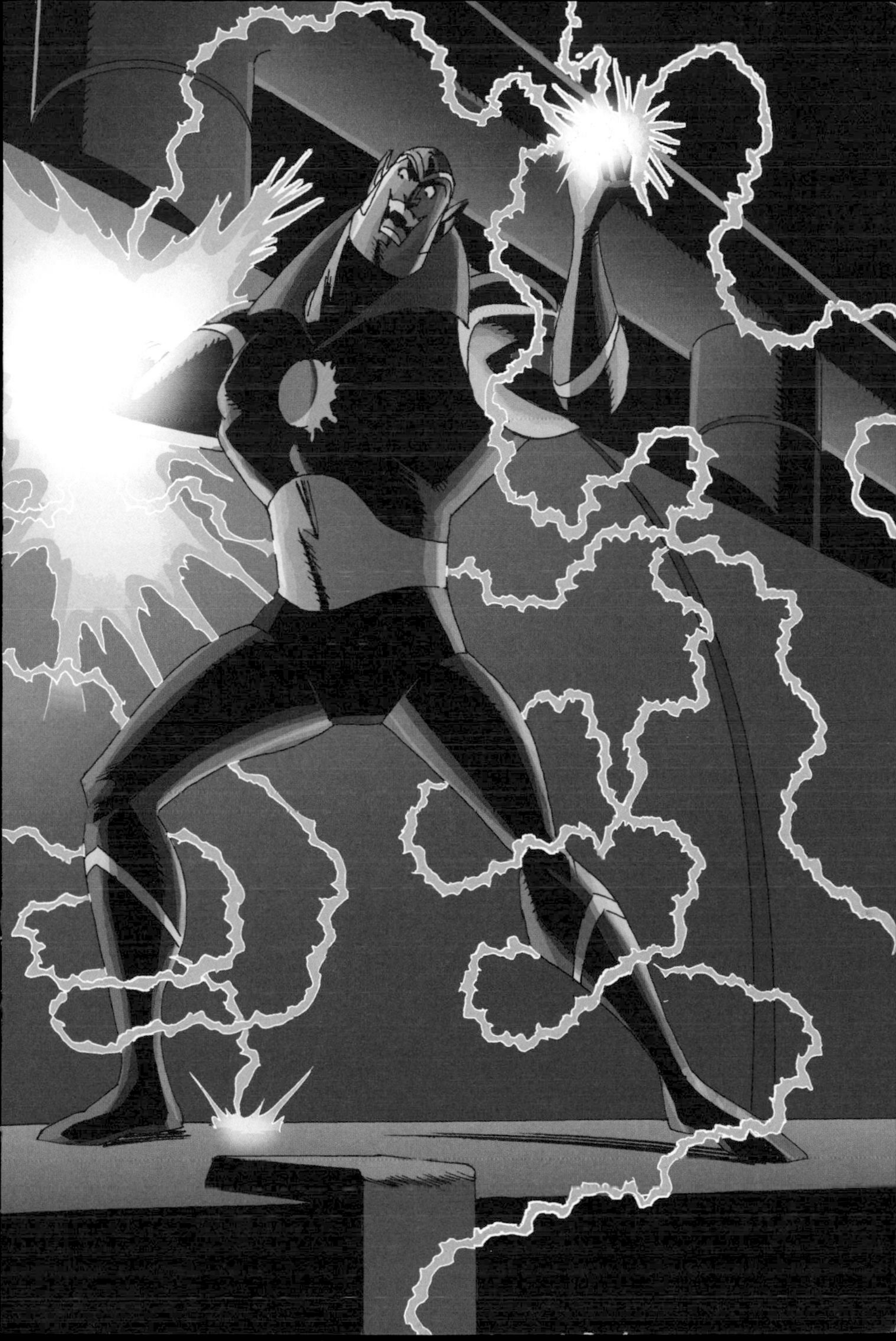

CHAPTER 5

POWER SURGE

Faster than a speeding bullet, the Man of Steel flew across the floor of the power plant. **KA-POW!** He slammed into the electrified form of the evil Eclipso.

The super-villain cried out in surprise. Eclipso's hand was pulled from the power of the giant turbine. Superman grabbed Eclipso's clenched fist in his own two hands.

"I said you're going back where you came from, Eclipso," Superman shouted. "And I meant it."

"I'm sure you did," Eclipso said. A spark of electricity danced in his black eyes. "Except you forgot one thing, Superman. My powers are magical!"

A black light erupted from between Eclipso's closed fingers. Eclipso stood up a little taller. He began to grow a little larger. When he laughed, it was a horrible, chilling sound. It rumbled from deep within his massive chest. Then he flicked his wrist and shook Superman loose.

"Oof!" Superman said, stumbling back.

The Man of Steel gained his mighty abilities from the energy of Earth's sun. He was like a human battery. His body stored the solar energy that gave him his many superpowers. When charged by the yellow sun's rays, Superman could not be hurt or harmed by most things.

However, the Man of Steel did have two weaknesses. One was green kryptonite, a radioactive rock from his destroyed home planet of Krypton. The other was *magic*!

Eclipso opened his fist. The black light spread around his arm, pulsing slowly. The dozens of pieces of black diamonds had started to dissolve. More power was needed to completely destroy the diamonds. Then Eclipso would have horrible, dark powers.

Superman filled his lungs with air. He blew ice toward the smoldering diamonds. **WHODDOSH!** He hoped it would stop the diamonds from melting.

ZZRRRRTT! The freezing air touched the rough chunks of black diamonds in Eclipso's hand. The cold air had little effect on the glowing rocks.

Eclipso clenched his fist again. A blast of dark energy burst from his hand. Superman leaped to one side to avoid the attack. But the magical energy simply followed him. Superman soared into the air. He flew toward the ceiling, speeding just ahead of the deadly blast. Then he looped back down toward Eclipso.

WHAM! Both Superman and the powerful energy blast hit Eclipso from above! The Shadow Man screamed. The impact drove the villain through the thick concrete floor.

Superman tried once more to wrestle the black diamonds from Eclipso's grasp.

"I went through too much trouble to gather these," Eclipso said. "You will not take them from me!"

Another blast of energy exploded from Eclipso's fist. ZZRRRRRTTT! It was powerful enough to send Superman tumbling back into the wall of the power plant.

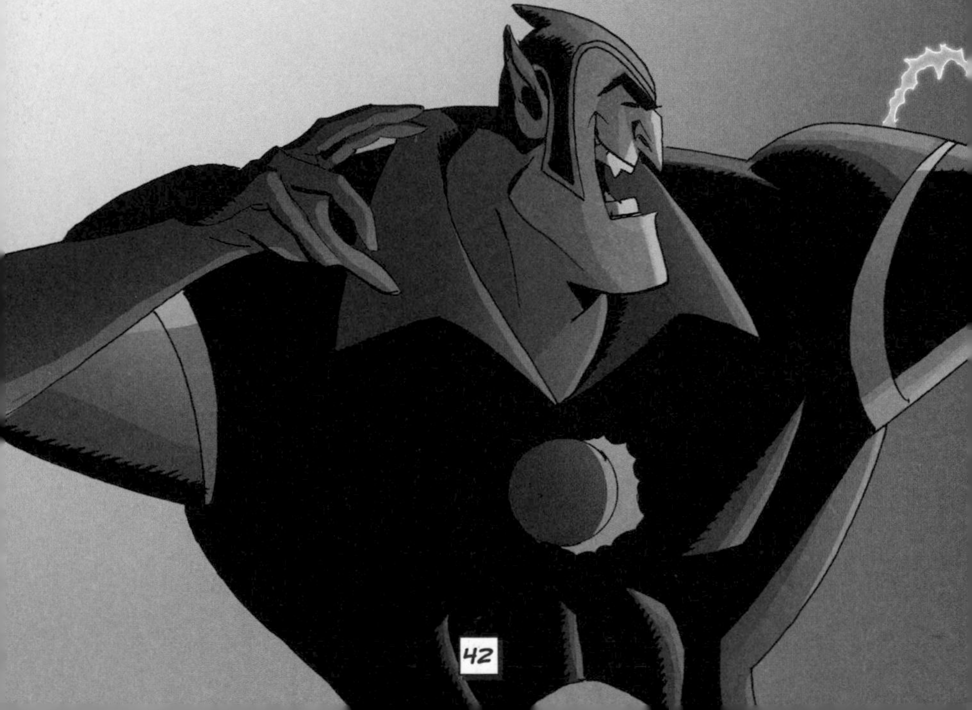

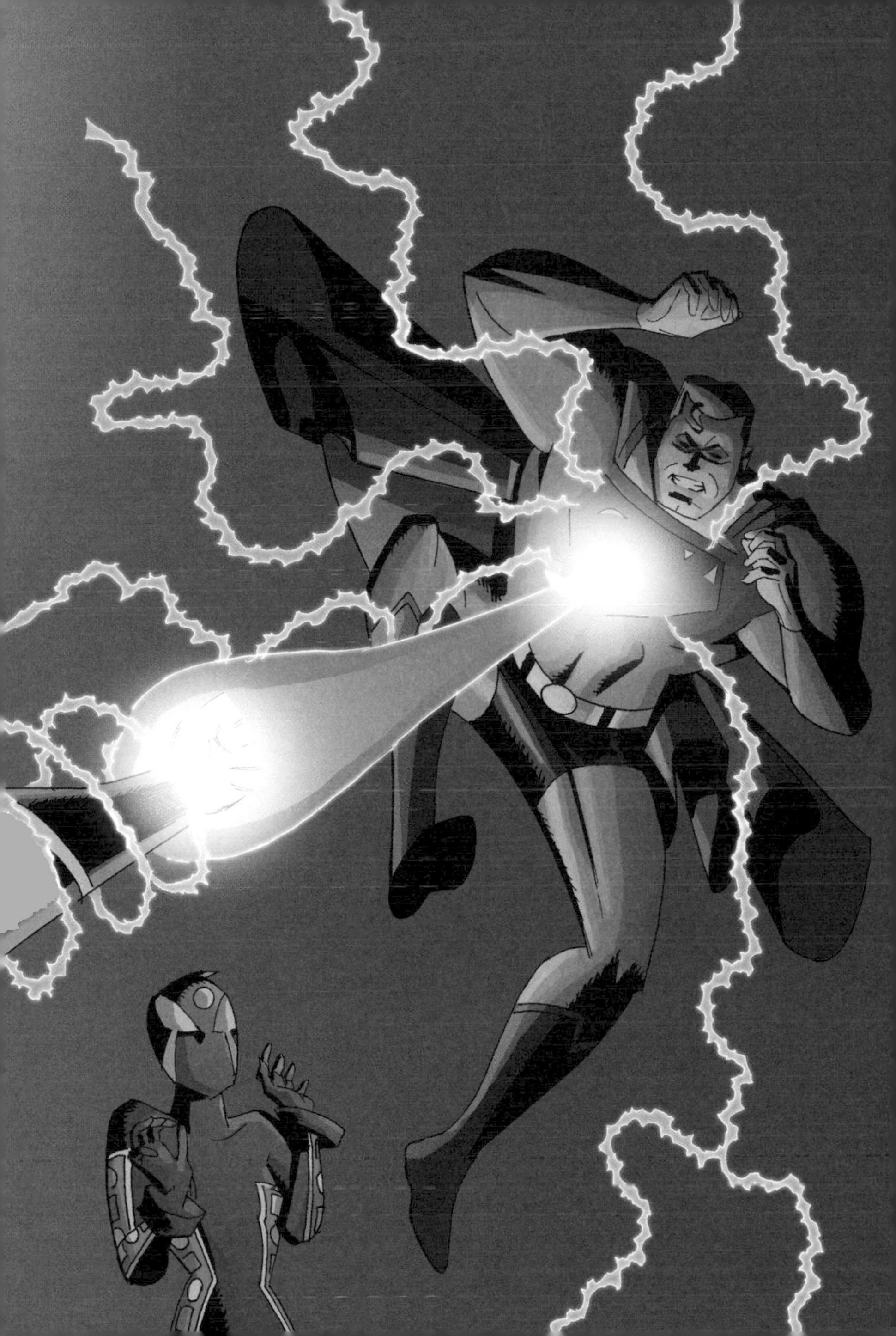

THUD! Superman landed next to the turbine. He tried to stand up. Instead, he collapsed in a heap.

He wasn't moving.

"No more interruptions!" Eclipso said, climbing from the hole. "I will get back to making this world my own kingdom of darkness."

Superman looked up and smiled.

"Now, Acrata!" the Man of Steel called out. "Shut it down!"

Eclipso turned to see Acrata. She was standing on a platform behind a large control console. It was covered with blinking lights and switches. One large, red button was under a plastic cover. Acrata lifted the cover. She stood with her finger an inch above it.

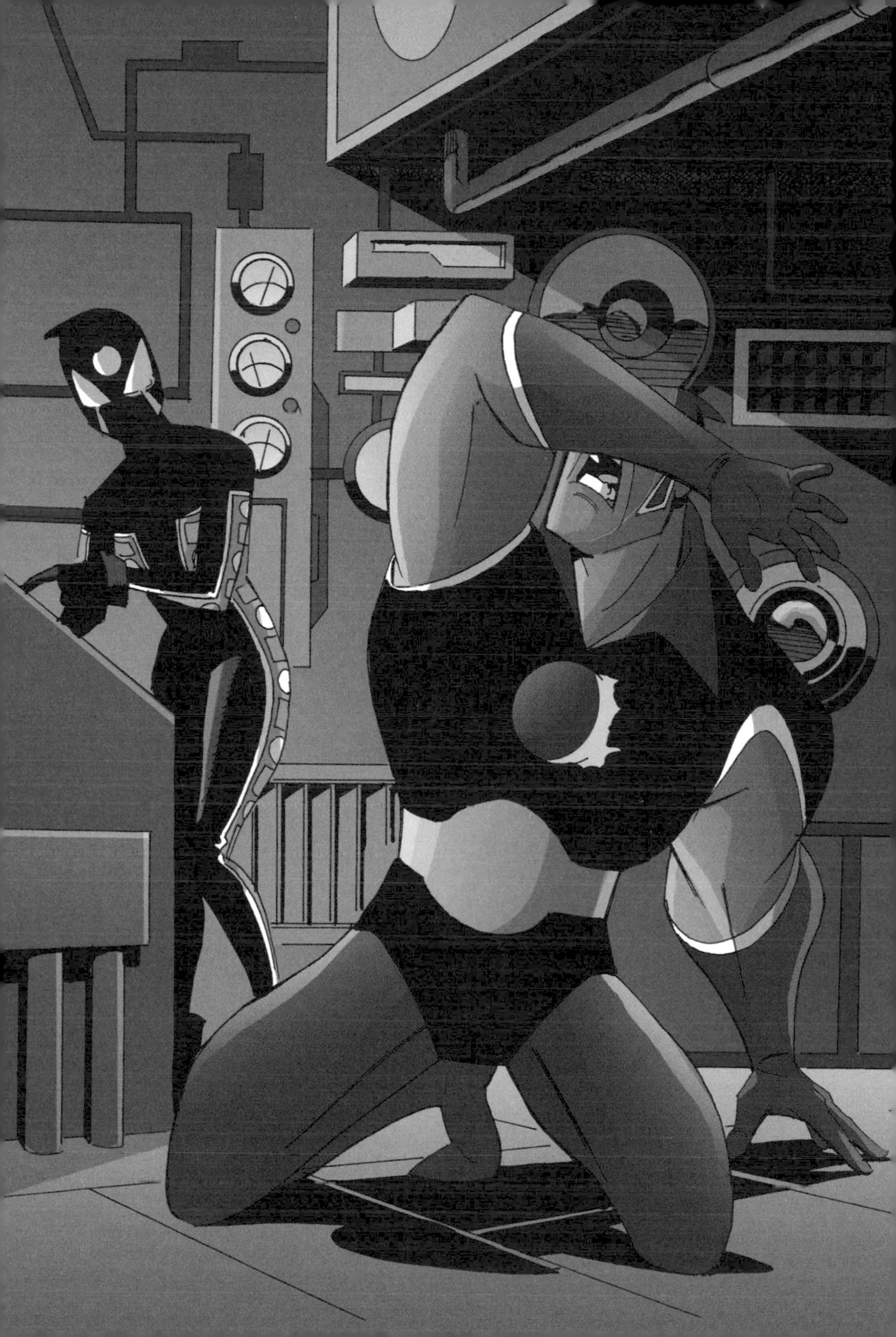

"*Adios,* Eclipso," she said. **CLICK!**
Acrata pushed the red button.

"No!" Eclipso screamed. It was an emergency button. He knew that it shut off the entire plant's power.

The turbines immediately ground to a stop. All the lights blinked out. The power plant was now in total darkness.

Superman leaped to his feet. He could hear the sounds of a scuffle in the darkness. First came Acrata's grunts of effort. Then came Eclipso's angry roar.

A moment later, the emergency lights flickered on. Only Superman and Acrata stood in the silent power plant. Scattered across the floor at their feet were pieces of black diamonds.

"Good work, Acrata," Superman said.

"I saw you were headed for the control panel," Superman said. "So I kept Eclipso distracted until you could reach the switch."

"And once we were in total darkness," agreed Acrata, "it was easy for me to drag Eclipso back into the shadows. I made him leave his rocks behind, however. He won't be escaping anytime soon!"

"I'll make sure to hide these diamonds," Superman said. "Now, he'll never be able to destroy them."

"We make a good team, Superman," Acrata said.

"We could have been an even better team," Superman added, "if you had kept me informed."

The two super heroes exited the power plant together.

The solar eclipse was nearly complete. Only a small sliver of the Moon's shadow remained.

"I'm sorry, Superman," Acrata said. "I was frightened by the Man in the Shadows."

"It all worked out this time," Superman said with a smile. "But if something like this ever happens again . . ."

"Yes, Superman," Acrata said. "Next time, I will not keep you in the dark!"

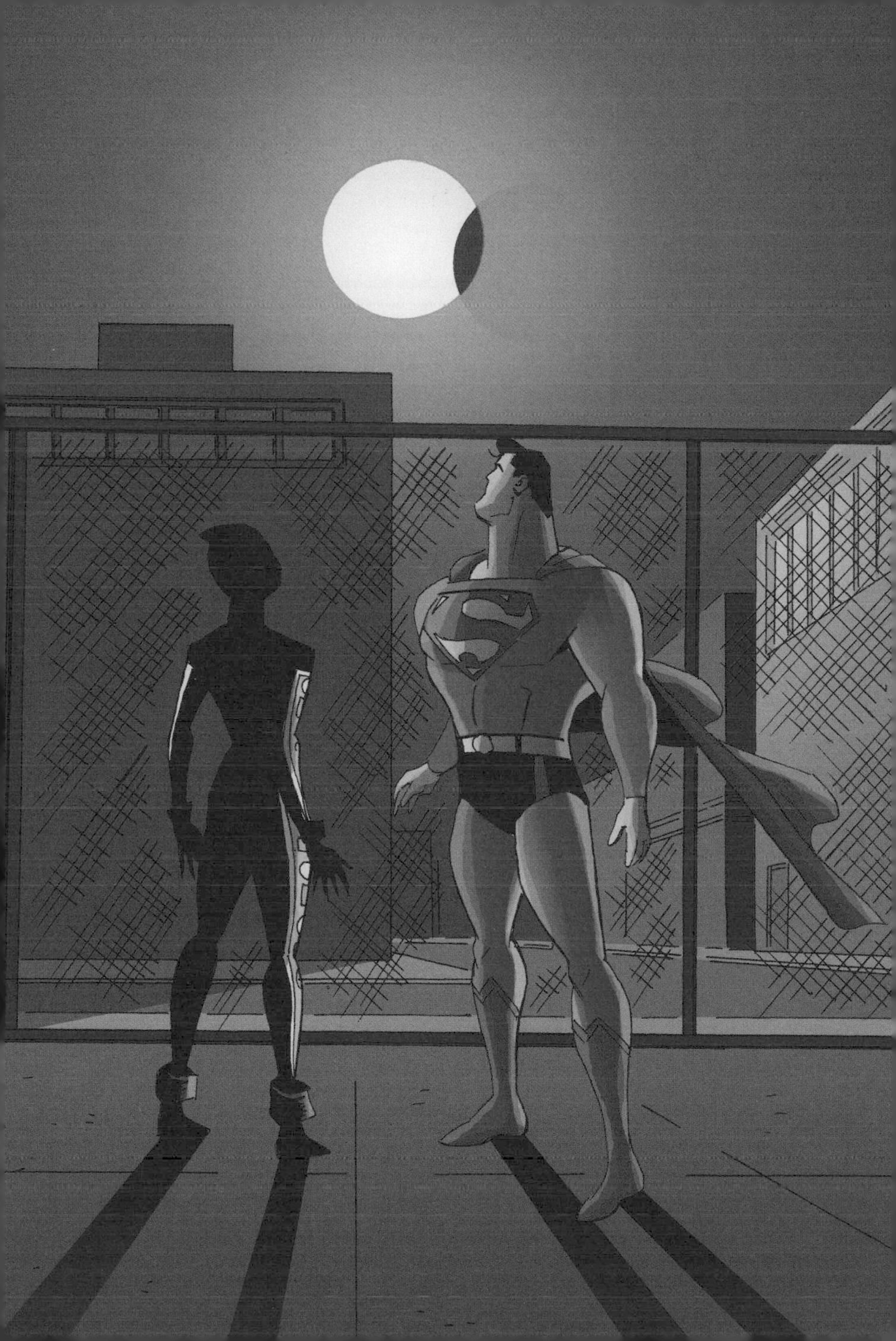

DAILY PLANET

FROM THE DESK OF CLARK KENT

WHO IS ACRATA?

During daylight, Andrea Rojas seems to be normal. She lives in Mexico and works as an anthropologist. She has a pet cat named *Zapata*, which means "shoe" in Spanish. When night falls, she becomes Acrata, striking at criminals by teleporting through the night. An ancient Maya symbol on her forehead allows Acrata to travel through the shadows as if they were doors. This ability, along with her impressive fighting skills, makes criminals afraid of their own shadows.

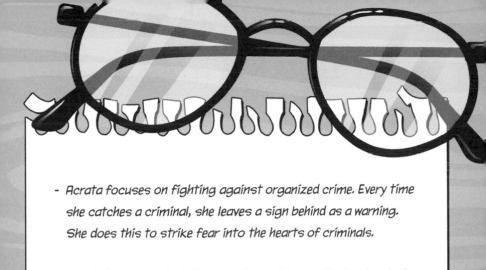

- Acrata focuses on fighting against organized crime. Every time she catches a criminal, she leaves a sign behind as a warning. She does this to strike fear into the hearts of criminals.

- Acrata has an ancient Maya symbol written on the forehead of her mask. The symbol stands for "shadows in the night," which grants her the ability to travel through the shadows. No one knows how Rojas came into possession of the symbol.

- Acrata has teamed up with the Man of Steel on more than one occasion. The two super heroes once worked together to save Mexico from a group of bio-terrorists.

- Acrata's father was a famous researcher at a Mexican university. He focused on helping his fellow citizens — a mission that Acrata herself continues.

BIOGRAPHIES

Paul Kupperberg has written many books for kids, like *Wishbone: The Sirian Conspiracy*, *Powerpuff Girls: Buttercup's Terrible Temper Tantrums*, and *Hey, Sophie!* Paul has also written over 600 comic book stories starring Superman, the Justice League, Batman, Wonder Woman, The Simpsons, Archie and Jughead, Scooby Doo, and many, many others Paul's own character creations include Arion: Lord of Atlantis, Checkmate, and Takion. He has also been an editor for DC Comics, Weekly World News, and World Wrestling Entertainment.

Rick Burchett has worked as a comics artist for more than 25 years. He has received the comics industry's Eisner Award three times, Spain's Haxtur Award, and he has been nominated for England's Eagle award. Rick lives with his wife and two sons near St. Louis, Missouri.

Lee Loughridge has been working in comics for more than fifteen years. He currently lives in sunny California in a tent on the beach.

GLOSSARY

ancient (AYN-shunt)—very old, or from long ago

artifacts (ART-uh-faktz)—objects made by ancient human beings, like tools or weapons

haze (HAYZ)—smoke, dust, or something else in the air that prevents you from seeing far

interfered (in-tur-FEERD)—hindered or prevented something or someone else

shattered (SHAT-urd)—broken into tiny pieces, or ruined completely

slither (SLITH-ur)—slip and slide like a snake

solar eclipse (SOH-lur ee-KLIPS)—when the moon comes between the sun and the earth, blocking out the sun's light

sorcerer (SOR-sur-er)—a wizard, or a male who performs or uses magic

turbine (TUR-bine)—an engine driven by water, steam, or gas passing through a wheel

ultimate (UHL-tuh-mit)—last or final, or greatest and best

DISCUSSION QUESTIONS

1. Acrata can teleport through the shadows. Superman can soar through the air. Which superpower would you rather have? Why?

2. Acrata didn't tell the Man of Steel what was going on at first. Is it ever okay to hide the truth from someone?

3. Who did more to stop Eclipso — Superman or Acrata? Why?

WRITING PROMPTS

1. Superman tried to stop Acrata because he didn't know that she was trying to save the world. Have you ever made a mistake? What happened? Write about your mistake.

2. How would our world be different if super-villains and super heroes existed?

3. Create your own super hero. Give him or her a name, a personality, some superpowers, and a secret identity. Then, draw a picture of your crime fighter.

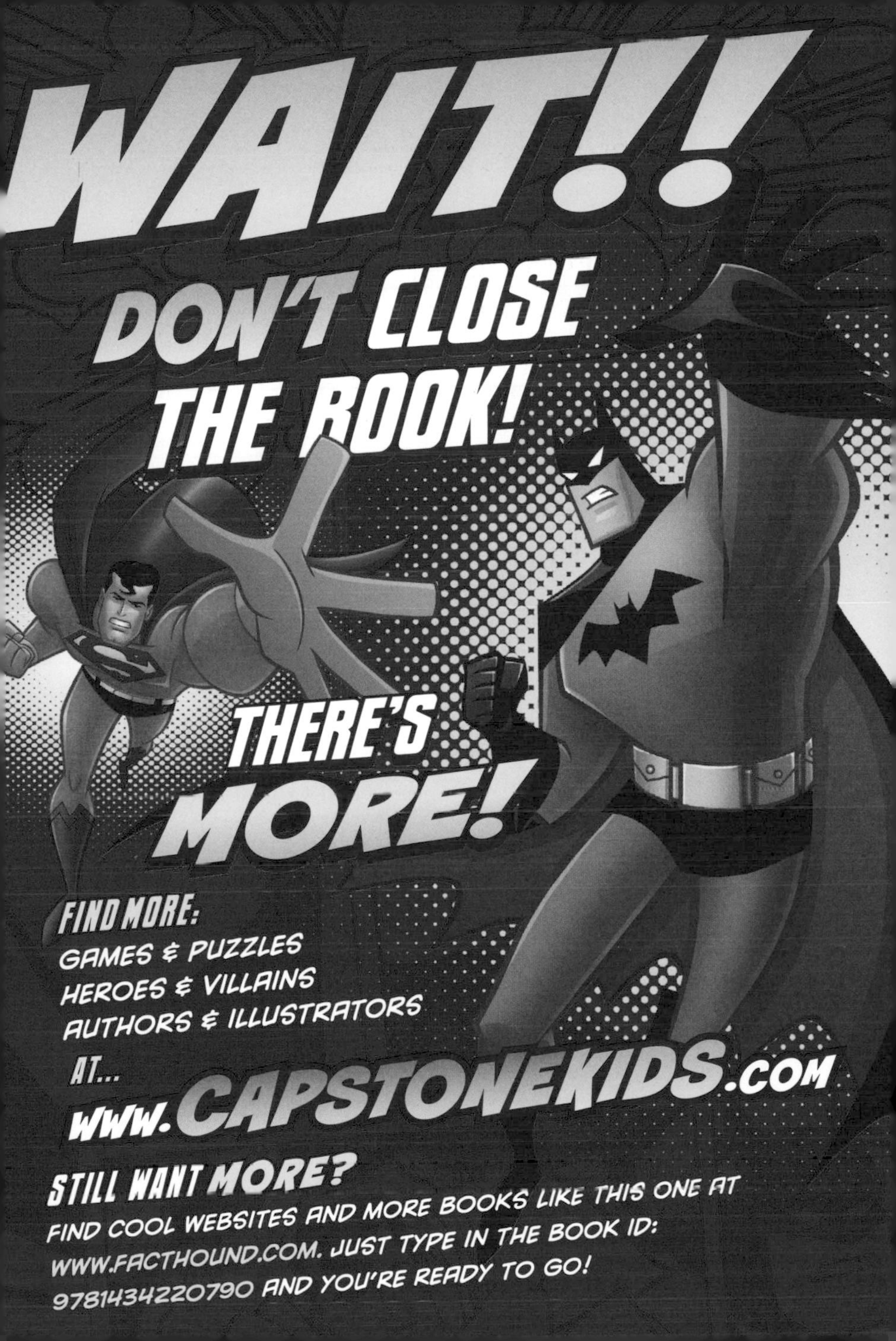
WAIT!!
DON'T CLOSE THE BOOK!
THERE'S MORE!
FIND MORE:
GAMES & PUZZLES
HEROES & VILLAINS
AUTHORS & ILLUSTRATORS
AT...
WWW.CAPSTONEKIDS.COM
STILL WANT MORE?
FIND COOL WEBSITES AND MORE BOOKS LIKE THIS ONE AT
WWW.FACTHOUND.COM. JUST TYPE IN THE BOOK ID:
9781434220790 AND YOU'RE READY TO GO!

MORE NEW SUPERMAN ADVENTURES!

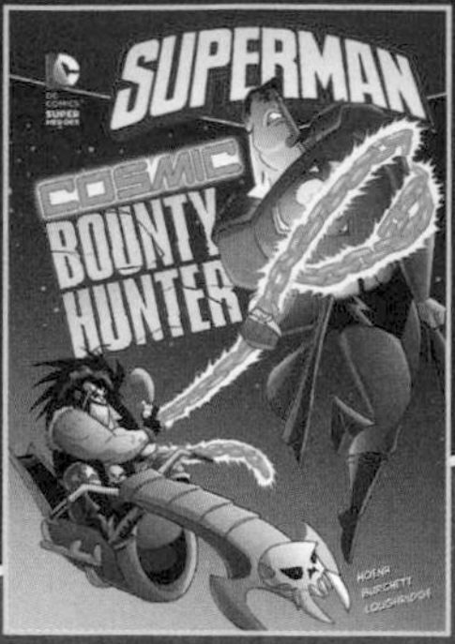
SUPERMAN
COSMIC
BOUNTY
HUNTER

COSMIC BOUNTY HUNTER

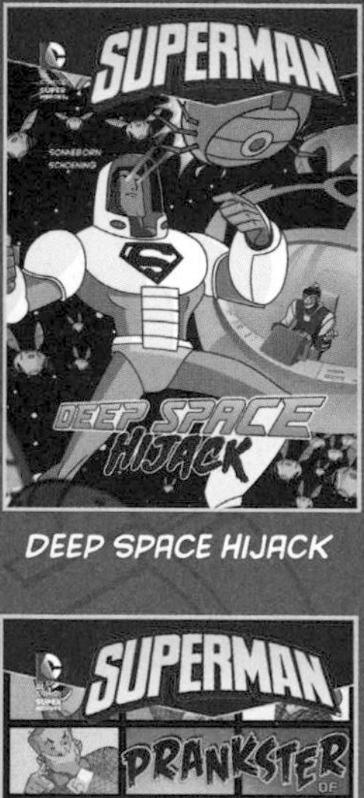
SUPERMAN
DEEP SPACE
HIJACK

DEEP SPACE HIJACK

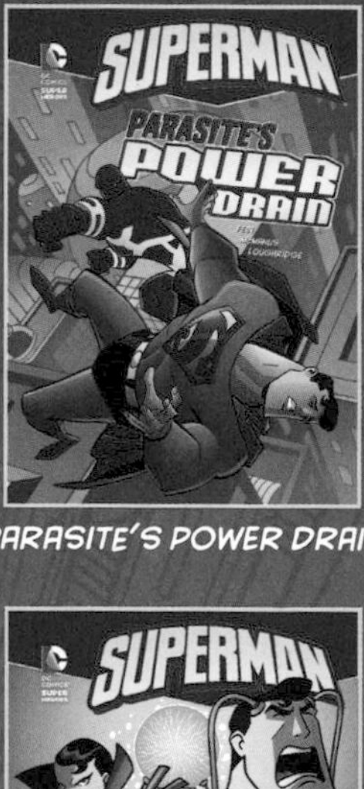
SUPERMAN
PARASITE'S
POWER
DRAIN

PARASITE'S POWER DRAIN

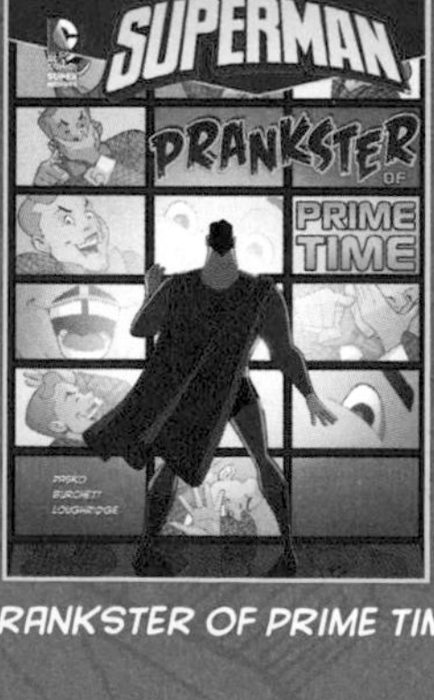
SUPERMAN
PRANKSTER
OF
PRIME
TIME

PRANKSTER OF PRIME TIME

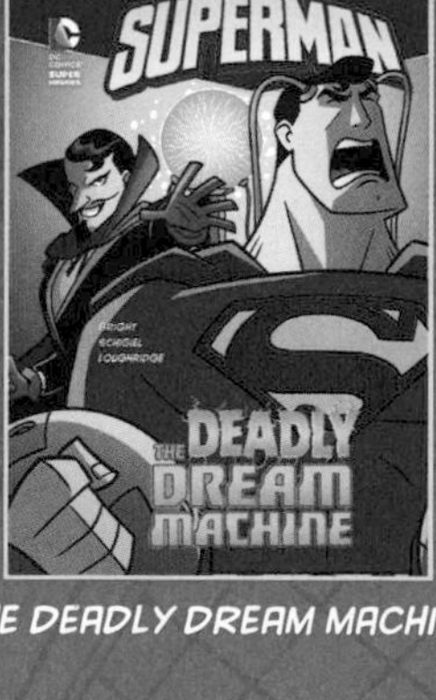
SUPERMAN
THE
DEADLY
DREAM
MACHINE

THE DEADLY DREAM MACHINE